The Man on the Bench
by
Cassie Light Redfeather

Copyright 2024. Cassie Light Redfeather. All Rights Reserved. No part of this book may be reproduced, in whole or in part, in print, audio, digital, electronic or any other format without first obtaining express written permission from the author. Copyright Act of 1976.

This book is dedicated to many people. First of all, it is for Chad—the man who changed my life forever and the man who said "I do!"

It is for my precious mother whose life I was privileged to share for more than ten and a half years. It was an extraordinary journey with a woman of great faith, of holiness, of resilience and courage. I am so proud to be her daughter.

For Prissy Britches—my beloved sister and friend—whose "courage under fire" is a testament to anyone of grace and faith—and of the ability to overcome the worst of obstacles.

It is for a man named "Colonel" who was a homeless vet and whose life marked mine with his story.

And this book is for two extraordinary men whose lives were cut short way too soon but nevertheless, they changed **my life** forever...

Jerry Sanders (August 2nd, 1965 – August 15, 2024)

David "The Saint" Clevinger (October 24, 1964 – September 5, 2024).

They believed in my work and that my books would one day change the world. I'll see you guys on the other side.

THE MAN ON THE BENCH

"FOR GOD, WHO COMMANDED the light to shine out of darkness, hath shined in our hearts, to give the light of the knowledge of the glory of God in the face of Jesus Christ."

2 Corinthians 4:6

Chapter One

My life was a mess. *How had everything gotten so out of control?* I didn't know—all I *did* know was that I was miserable and unhappy, caught up in a life going nowhere.

Don't ask me why I took to going to the park every Sunday. I started going about five weeks ago. I drank my cup of morning joe, black and strong, scrolled through the depressing news of my daily newspaper, took a two-mile jog, changed into a new pair of sweats and walked to the park.

I worked seventy-hour weeks at a job I hated, could not remember the last time I'd had a vacation, was in over my head with debt and still wondered—*what was my purpose? How in hell do I get out of this mess?*

The park was lovely this time of year, autumn, with the leaves a beautiful rustic shade and it was the one time in my life that I felt like I could really breathe fresh air and see the sky instead of the damn skyscrapers surrounding my apartment.

For some reason, on this particular Sunday, I started to weep. I would just look at a sky so beautiful and perfect, then tears flowed down my face.

When I looked up, I found myself staring into the face of what could only be a homeless man, pushing a cart up to the bench where I sat.

"Mind if I sit here," he said, motioning to the seat next to me on the bench.

Startled, I said, "No."

He sat down next to me and when I looked into his face, I stared into the most beautiful blue eyes, sculpted like crisp blue ice, only filled with a warmth and fire that was hard to explain.

"Come here often," he asked, staring at me with those eyes.

"Every Sunday."

"I see. On the Lord's Day," he said quietly.

"Well, I hadn't thought of it like that," I replied, "but I guess it is."

"Ain't no guessing to it. It *is* the Lord's Day."

There was a determination to his voice when he said that his voice resonating with quiet strength.

"Well, okay, you're right," I conceded, "it *is* the Lord's Day."

"Yep. You'd be right about that. What's your name?"

"Katie Ellen Winthrop."

"Nice to meet you, Katie Ellen."

"What's your name?"

"I didn't say," he said with a smile.

"Well, don't you have a name," I asked.

"Yes, I do have a name. We all have a name," he said quietly.

"Well," I said again, "will you tell me your name?"

"Yes, I will, but only when it's time for me to tell you. Until then, it will be my little secret," he said with a chuckle.

There was a magnetic warmth to this homeless man.

"Okay. I won't ask again," I said, "but how long have you been homeless?"

"What makes you think I'm homeless?"

"Well, you are, aren't you?"

"You sure ask a lot of questions Katie Ellen. To most people, yes, it would appear that I am a homeless man. Been homeless a long time."

"Why?"

"There are more reasons than I can tell you right now about why I'm homeless—but in due time I think I will tell you. If you come here every Sunday, I promise I'll show up, too."

"Okay."

"What troubles you?" he asked with that quiet inquisitiveness that commanded my attention—and those blue eyes, piercing into the soul I didn't even think I had.

"My life."

"How so?"

"I'm in so much trouble I don't know what to do!" I blurted out. "I hate my job, I work all the time, I never rest and I'm up to my eyeballs in debt. Everywhere I turn it's always a slammed door."

"Doors slam for a reason, Katie Ellen. Sometimes doors slam to push you to the open door and then you only have to turn the lock when it's the open door."

Those words sent shivers down my spine.

"I never had anyone say that to me. I can't get a door open no matter how hard I try."

"Maybe that's because you're trying to keep a door open that doesn't need to be open anymore," he said quietly before continuing, "but maybe you're afraid to open a new door because of what's waiting on the other side. Everybody has a purpose, Katie Ellen, even you."

I gasped when he said that. *How could he know? I'd been searching for my purpose, whatever it was, for so long.*

"You live near skyscrapers," he asked.

How did he know that? The hair stood up on my arm. "I do."

"You see, Katie Ellen, those skyscrapers hide the sky from you. It's a blockage. The sky can't reach you because the skyscrapers are in the way."

"I don't know why you showed up this morning. I've been coming here for five weeks and suddenly, here you are," I said and then smiled when I said it. "I'm glad you did, whoever you are."

"To you, for now, I'm just a homeless man. You've been needing answers for a long time."

Tears cascaded down my face again. I wiped the tears away. "I'm sorry," I said, "I didn't mean to cry."

"Tears are a good thing. Don't you know? *Tears are liquid prayers.*"

"Thank you. I mean, I don't even know why I'm thanking you but there's something tender and special about you."

He got up off the bench suddenly. "Here," he said, withdrawing something from his pocket and handing it to me.

"What is it," I said as he shoved something in my hands. I was staring at a five-dollar bill. "Five dollars?"

"Yes, Katie Ellen. To most that's all it is, just a five-dollar bill but I tell you what. I'll be back here next Sunday at this bench, the same time. Tell me what you do with the five dollars next week, okay? I've got to go now, but I'll be here, same time at the bench. Don't you miss our date," he said with a chuckle.

He got up, pushed his cart and I watched him until his back was not more than a shadow some five minutes later as he disappeared around the trees shading the park on the north side.

I stared down at the five-dollar bill in my hand.

Five dollars from a homeless man.

Chapter Two

*T*hree days later I was still staring at that five-dollar bill every time I opened my purse at my job.

There was a different feel to this money and yet, it bothered me. *What was I supposed to do with it?*

I truly didn't know.

ON SUNDAY, I FOUND myself back at the park headed toward the bench and there he was! He was waiting for me, sitting on the bench his cart by his side.

What was it about this man? Why had he shown up in my life and how was I going to explain that I still had the five-dollar bill in my pocket?

As it turns out, I didn't have to explain it to him.

He spoke before I did. "You still got the five-dollar bill, don't you?"

"How did you know?"

"It don't matter how I know, but you still got it, don't you?"

I shuffled my feet for some uneasy reason and looked down at the ground.

"Well?" he pressed.

"Well," I said. That's about all I could manage. I had no idea why I was hesitating to tell him about a five-dollar bill still in my pocket. I mean it was just a five-dollar bill. *How important could it be?*

"You didn't answer my question," he persisted.

"Yes, I still have it," I replied.

"Why?"

He was full of questions even though most of them were one-word questions.

"I don't *know why*. I just didn't know what to do with it."

His eyes were not condemning, rather they were filled with something so powerful, like they were searching for my soul, but in a way that was filled with unfathomable love.

"You have a hard week?"

"All of my weeks are hard weeks," I said with a sigh and the rest came rushing out of my mouth. "*I am so unhappy.*"

"Then why don't you change it?"

"What?"

"Are you hard of hearing," he said with a smile, "I said why don't you change it?"

"Because I don't know how."

"Here," he said, standing up to his full height, which seemed to me was about six feet or so. "Let me show you something."

He let go of the cart and took a few steps in the opposite direction and turned back to look at me, "Now, tell me, what did I just do?"

"Well, you got up off the bench and took a few steps."

"Getting up was the first step."

"Okay."

"Taking the actual steps was the next thing."

"What are we, life lessons 101?"

"No," he said quietly as he sat back down again, those blue eyes filled with humility and *that was it!* Peace.

"Go on with what you were saying," I continued.

"You see, I had to get up off this bench. The longer I sat here the more I would come to a standstill. I can't take a step while I'm sitting down. Then I had to put my feet to work for me and push them in a direction one way or the other."

"I see."

"Do you really," he said quietly. "Katie, no decision *is* a decision. And in life if you stay stuck in neutral you won't ever go anywhere. Reverse leads you to yesterday. Drive sends you forward. You've spent too much time stuck in neutral and you're afraid, Katie."

A shiver went down my spine again when he uttered those words. *How was it this man knew so much about my life and consequently, my soul?*

"Do you want to tell me your name?" I asked.

"No."

"Why not?"

"Because if I told you my name you wouldn't believe me—at least not yet. When the time is right I'll tell you and by then maybe you'll believe me."

"Why did you show up at this bench?"

"Because I was supposed to."

Maddening! Absolutely maddening! However, I meant that in a good way. "Well, what are we supposed to do? Keep meeting at the park?"

"I will be here for as long as I need to be, Katie. You've been in trouble a long time."

Those damn hot tears flooded my face again!

"Liquid prayers," he reminded me gently. "Trouble comes and trouble goes, Katie but in life there will always be storms. It's how you handle the storms that matter."

"I don't seem to know how to get out of this place in my life and I don't know how to make a change."

He got up off the bench again and pointed with his finger towards the sky, "One step, Katie. One step. That's all it takes. Faith as small as a grain of a mustard seed moves mountains."

"Sometimes when you don't know where to go and what to do, just look up." He pointed to the sky again.

"How do I find my way," I blurted out. "I don't like my job, I hate the long hours and I don't like how I live."

"*Then you change it, Katie. You can't sit on the bench forever.*" And then his voice changed, "What moves you?"

"What do you mean?"

"What troubles you, Katie? What would you want your life to say about you?"

"Indifference bothers me," I replied without having to think about it. "And the plight of poor people."

"And why is that?" he continued calmly.

"People are just thrown away. I saw it with my mother and father. They didn't do anything wrong. *They just got old.*"

"How long ago did they pass?"

Those shivers shot up my arm again! My mother passed five years ago and my father had passed seven years ago. How in the world could he know that?

"Mama passed five years ago and Daddy passed seven years ago."

"You take care of them?"

"Yes," I said in a whisper.

"Working all those hours and burying yourself in debt help you forget your loss?"

"No," I said again with a floodgate of more tears on my face.

"You didn't lose them, Katie," he said with a whisper. "You just can't see them for a while. They're on a journey that is not yours to travel at this time."

I couldn't stop sobbing.

"Don't you know," he said gently.

"Know what," I managed to say between sobs.

"*You will be reunited.*"

When he said that it was like a dam bursting from somewhere inside my soul and all the pent-up emotions of caregiving, rebuilding my life and the trauma of my world being turned upside down came crashing down around me.

He didn't say anything for a few minutes, just let me sit there on the bench like a blubbering fool and then he spoke.

"You did the right thing, you know."

"About what?"

"Taking your mother off life support."

There was no way he could possibly have known that my mother had been critically ill for a long time and that I had made the excruciatingly painful decision for doctors to take her off life support.

"How did you know?"

"How I know is not so important as the lesson, Katie. If God had wanted your mother to live he didn't need ventilators and life support to keep her alive. After all, He is the one who created her."

I had never thought about it quite like that.

"It's not your fault," he said calmly.

"What's not my fault," I asked.

"Your mother's illness and all she went through. It's not your fault but you blame yourself. You been blaming yourself for a very long time."

"I have," I whispered.

"You know, Katie, the burden was never yours to carry. God was carrying that burden right along with you. The burden was His, not yours and He helped you carry it because the Cross is always on His shoulders. He's the one who carried it, you know."

With his words I remember not so much all the Sunday School lessons of my life but the resiliency, faith and courage of my mother who always said it best: *"Katie, fight your battles on your knees. Fight your battles with prayer."*

"It's like your mother told you, Katie. God is always with you. And you fight your battles on your knees."

"Who *are* you?"

"A homeless man pushing a cart."

"*I don't think so.*"

He smiled. "Maybe so. Maybe not. Katie, you can't go forward if you're always looking back. Your past is behind you and the future is in front of you."

"I know that."

"You know it in here," he said pointing to his temple, "but do you know it in here?" he continued pointing to his heart.

"Maybe I don't know it in my heart."

"You will. If indifference and poverty bother you so much then why don't you do something about it?"

"How can I do that? It's just me."

"Why do you think I gave you that five dollars?"

"Hell if I know," I blurted out before I thought about it.

"Hell doesn't want you to know the secret in those five dollars."

"I don't see how five dollars would bother hell."

"It bothers hell what you do with those five dollars."

"Oh."

"Katie, now look," he said, "hand me the five dollars."

"Okay," I said, taking it out of my pocket and handing it to him.

"You were afraid to do something with those five dollars. Fear blocks blessing and fear blocks doors."

"I never thought about it."

"If you think five dollars is all you have, then that's pretty much all you have. You care about poverty and the indifference in the world. If I'm homeless and have nothing, would five dollars help me have something to eat?"

I never thought of it like that. "Yeah," I managed to say when the truth of what he said hit me.

"If I'm a poor mother who doesn't have money for milk for her baby, would five dollars have bought her milk?"

"Yeah."

"Would five dollars show someone that you cared enough about their plight to help them with all you had?"

"Yeah."

"You see, five dollars is what's called a widow's mite. It don't look like much until you put it into the hands of someone who can use it."

"I think I'm beginning to understand."

"Five dollars is just five dollars as long as it's in your hand," he said, "Here," he continued as he shoved the five dollars back in my hand. "Come back next Sunday."

Again, he got up off the bench, headed in the same direction, only this time he looked at the sky and waved before rounding the corner.

Chapter Three

It's a funny thing about this Sunday morning routine at the bench. It was getting to be a regular habit. I showed up the next Sunday and there he was.

"You been here long," I asked when I got there.

"Yep."

"You don't mince words, do you?"

"Not if I can help it. How was your week, Katie?"

"Better than the ones before it. Aren't you gonna ask me about that five-dollar bill?"

"Nope."

I was amazed. "Why not?"

"I'm not gonna ask you about it right now. That's all."

"Why do you come here every Sunday to meet me on the bench?"

"I came because you need me, Katie."

"What?"

"You always want me to repeat things," he said with a smile. "I came because you need me.

A light misting rain started. "Uh oh," I said with a laugh, "we won't have much time on the bench."

"Maybe not." He pulled something from his pocket. "This what you do with the five-dollar bill?"

I was stunned. There was my envelope with my handwriting on it because I'd mailed it as a donation. "How did you get that?"

"That's not for you to know, Katie. Why did you mail it?"

"Uh," I thought for an excuse. "I just, uh, mailed a donation."

"Is there anyone around that needs food," he asked.

"I don't know."

"Well, why don't you find out," he answered, handing me back my envelope. "Come back next week and tell me if you found someone that was hungry." With that statement, he got up, pushed his cart and headed in a different direction. "Same time, same place next Sunday, Katie." He smiled and nodded. Those eyes! How did they have a peace that I never knew how to find?

Chapter Four

Often the truth is in places where we least expect to see it and I saw it because of the five-dollar bill.

I had grown to love going to the park and finding my friend, whoever he is.

This Sunday was a bit of a surprise as I approached the bench, ready to tell him what I did with the five-dollar bill.

He wasn't there!

Where could he be?

My eyes searched the perimeter, and I didn't see him.

I sat down on the bench to wait. Within a few minutes a man came up to me in a blue suit, a felt hat pulled down towards his eyes.

"Mind if I sit here?"

Odd, I thought. What *is* it with these strange men sitting with me at the bench?

"Nope."

He sat down.

It wasn't until he pulled his hat off that I recognized him. *It was him!*

"What happened to you? You don't—"

"I don't look like me?" He said with a laugh.

"No, you don't. Did you get a job?"

He laughed again. "I already had a job when we met."

"Then why are you dressed so differently?"

"Does how I look matter, Katie?"

"No."

"Looks matter to the world. People often judge people by how they look, like that adage *"don't judge a book by its cover"*. What people are and who they are isn't dependent on how they dress."

"Are you still homeless?"

"I'm homeless when I need to be."

"You don't give away much information about yourself, do you," I added with my own laugh.

"No more than is necessary."

"So, why the suit?"

"It's to show you something very important. Perception is like looking through a camera lens. What you see depends on what the camera reflects. Sometimes the lens makes it look one way and at other times you see something quite different, depending on the angle of the camera, the lighting and all that. Would you feel any differently about me now that I'm in a suit?"

"Not at all."

"Katie, every day people are judged by the car they drive, the house they live in and the money in their bank accounts when none of that really matters at all."

"It doesn't matter."

"But to some people it does. Have you ever noticed that people sometimes think a person *has it all* when they see the house the person lives in or the car the person drives or the job title someone holds?"

"Yes, I see what you mean."

"Sometimes what we see on the outside is a disguise for what's really going on inside. How many times have you discovered someone is miserable when, to the outside world, it looks like they have it all?"

"Quite a lot, actually."

"People treat me differently if they see me in rags, pushing a cart and to the world, perception is everything. They judge what they cannot see and they condemn that which they do not know. Katie, condemnation and judgment is destroying people all over the world."

"I think so."

"In rags I'm just a homeless man pushing a cart and most people think I'm homeless and in rags because of drugs and alcohol or bad choices. They forget there are so many real reasons underneath the rags."

"There's always a reason for everything. Mama taught me that."

He smiled. "She had beautiful brown eyes, your Mama did."

Tears pooled in my eyes. Mama's eyes were a beautiful chocolate brown and once again, *how did he know that?* I've learned not to ask.

"Yes, she did."

"What lies underneath the rags are often people that are, as you say, thrown away and left to die on the street because housing was too high, or there wasn't a job with high enough wages. It's a complicated thing but in God's eyes, *we are all God's people.*"

"I have to agree with you on that one, too." I was actually agreeing with him on a lot of things.

"So, did Alicia get her gallon of milk with your five-dollar bill?"

"I know better than to ask you how you knew that. She works with me and she doesn't make much money. Her baby is two years old. I gave her the money to buy milk for her baby."

"Do you know what that five-dollar bill became?"

"An answer to a prayer?"

"Yes, and even though it was a gallon of milk it was a lifeline for her—a lifeline of hope. She was beginning to wonder if anyone ever heard her prayers. She prays all the time because she doesn't have enough money for food or milk for her baby."

"Oh." It seemed like that's what I always replied but honestly, I was beginning to be in awe of this man, whoever he really is.

"Looks can be deceiving, Katie. People aren't always what they're wrapped up to be. And sometimes people have needs that others don't know about."

"That's true."

"Do you know what Alicia did with the little bit of change from your five-dollar bill?"

"I have no idea. She couldn't have had much change left from it."

"Forty-eight cents."

"I am not about to ask how you know that," I said with a smile. "There's not much anyone can do with forty-eight cents."

"Alicia didn't look at it that way. She took the forty-eight cents and added the only two cents she had left to her name and she gave it away to someone that needed a loaf of bread."

"Fifty cents wouldn't buy a loaf of bread."

"No, it won't but the person she gave it to had $1.78 in change and was praying for a loaf of bread."

"Oh." Why was that all I seemed to say when I was around him?

"You see, Katie, that five dollars was just five dollars in your hand but once it left your hand, it took on a life of its own. Alicia got a gallon of milk and her friend got a loaf of bread. Wanna know what her friend did with her loaf of bread?"

"Yes, I do."

"She took half the loaf and gave it to her elderly neighbor who had two weeks to go before her pension check arrived and was already out of bread."

"I had no idea five dollars would go so far."

"It's what you call a twice-sown seed."

"What did the elderly woman do with the half loaf of bread?"

"She made a pot of soup and shared one slice of bread with a bowl of soup to a friend who'd been sick for a while."

"And what happened next?"

"The woman that was sick took half the bowl of soup and added beans and rice to it to make a larger meal then she shared half of that with a homeless man lingering on the street near her home."

"I never thought my five dollars would touch so many lives."

"That's because it was never your five dollars to begin with. It was God's. He took what seemed to be so little and turned it into something greater than the sum total of its parts."

He pulled something out of his pocket. "Here you go, Katie." He handed me a watch. "Study that watch until next Sunday and let me know what it teaches you."

He lingered for a few minutes with that smile of radiance on his face and then he got up off the bench one more time and headed back behind the trees, waving as he did so.

I stared at the watch and put it in my purse.

Chapter Five

I looked forward to Sundays on the bench now. If you really want to know the truth, they had become my favorite part of the week.

Sunday came and went this time and my friend didn't show. I waited for two hours, and he wasn't there. Perplexed, puzzled and somehow disheartened I left the park only to return the next Sunday and there he was, sitting on the bench like he hadn't missed the last Sunday.

"You weren't here last Sunday," I said.

"So you noticed, hmm?" He said with a smile.

"Why weren't you there?" I noticed a hammer in his hand and a chisel. *What in the world?*

"Been a little busy," he replied with that same smile.

"Okay. Aren't you gonna ask me about the watch?"

"Nope. It's not time to ask you about it. You still got it."

"Yes, I do."

"I'll ask you about the watch when it's time to do so. No pun intended," he added with a laugh.

"What in the world are you doing with a hammer and a chisel?"

"I see you know what they are but then you would. Your father was a carpenter, at least during the daytime."

I should never be surprised at what he knew about me. "Yes, that's true, he was."

"He knew how to build houses."

"Yes, he did."

"However, he farmed at night after long days building and renovating houses." He took a pack of seed out of his pocket. "Here, Katie." He handed me the packet of seed. I was staring at tomato seeds.

"What in the world do you want me to do with the tomato seeds? I live in an apartment."

"I know you do, Katie, but that's not really all that important right now. What did your father do with seed?"

"He planted every seed in the ground."

"And how did he do that?"

"He put his hand to the plow, so to speak, and he did what farmers call "disked" up the field and then he dropped the seed in the ground."

"So he cultivated the soil, essentially, before he dropped the seed in the soil, right?"

"Yes, although I never really thought of it like that."

"There's more to it than that, you know."

"Yes, I guess there is. What is today, a lesson in farming and carpentry?" I asked with a smile.

"No, like I said, there's a little bit more to it than that."

"I thought so."

"First of all, your father had to know what kind of soil grows tomatoes, or whatever else he had to plant. Not all things grow the same way in the same soil."

"That's true."

"He had to know when to plant, how to plant, what type of soil to plant them in. For instance, you won't grow a darn thing if you plant it in sand. The sand will kill it!"

"You're a lost farmer in disguise," I said with a laugh.

"And you have to be careful how closely you plant things to each other. It's a tomatoes and gourds thing."

"A tomatoes and gourds thing?" I asked, puzzled and somewhat perplexed.

"If you want tomatoes, you don't plant gourds and if you plant tomatoes too close to the gourds, your crop won't be what you expected—or what you desired."

"I get it," I said with a laugh. "At least I think I do."

"Katie, life is like that soil. You plant your life for a reason, for a purpose. You're not born just to do what you want to do. You're here for a reason, a divine purpose. Your life is a seed, depending on what you do with it."

"You do surprise me," I said. "I never have been able to figure out my purpose. At least not yet."

"Oh, you know what your purpose is, you just haven't accepted it yet. And remember, Katie, you will never reap a harvest if you don't plant."

"It's hard to plant when you don't have anything to give," I said, feeling sadness well up inside of me as I said it.

"Is that what you think," he said with that radiant smile.

"I don't have much, at least in the way of what the world calls material goods."

"What you have, Katie, my dear, is your life. Your life is a seed. Don't you know that?"

"What?" His words startled me, although he was doing that a lot so it didn't surprise me, at least not this time.

"Money is to be respected and even money has a purpose, although it is sad to say, more people misuse it than those who know its purpose. Everything in your life is a seed. Every time you speak a kind word or commit an act of kindness, that's your seed. Every act of love is a gift to whoever receives it. Compassion is a gift planted into the life of someone else. You do that by your actions, Katie. Sometimes, your life is the only Bible anyone will ever read."

I don't know why this man made me cry but he'd done it again. Tears pouring down my face like a floodgate and they wouldn't stop.

"Nobody ever told me that."

"I know," he said softly and reached for my hand.

Radiant warmth spread through my hand when he touched it. *A healing touch.*

"I keep telling you. It's okay to cry. Tears are not only liquid prayers. Sometimes they cleanse the soul, you know."

"No, I didn't know," I said as I wiped the tears from my face.

"Never be ashamed to cry and don't you ever be ashamed to let someone see your tears."

"I won't."

"You promise me?" He said with a stern look suddenly appearing in those blue eyes.

"I promise."

"Now about this hammer and chisel in my hands," he said.

"What about them?"

"A hammer can build or destroy whatever it strikes, and a chisel carves something out of nothing. Here," he said, handing both of them to me. "Take them home with you and study them. Look closely at them and tell me next Sunday what you discovered."

"What about the watch," I persisted as I stared at the hammer and the chisel in my hands.

"When the time is right. Gotta go, Katie." He got up off the bench, waved with his hand and said, "See you next Sunday. Don't be late."

I watched him go around the same corner and there was an aura of light around him, something different that had not been there before.

I didn't know who he was, at least not yet, but all I *did* know was that five dollars from a homeless man was changing my life.

Chapter Six

It's a funny thing about this park and the bench. It was more than that now. I had been coming here so long that I no longer viewed it as I did when I first arrived.

This Sunday, my friend, whoever he is, was waiting for me on the bench, dressed in, of all things, a clown outfit.

"What in God's name are you doing in a clown outfit?" I said with a laugh.

"See," he said with a chuckle, "it already made you laugh. People need to laugh, Katie. There's too much sadness and sorrow in this world."

"That's true," I said laughing again, "but did you have to show up in a clown outfit to prove it?"

"Sometimes you have to make a statement to people and the only way to do that is to make them see something for what it actually is. People don't laugh. Humor heals, Katie. You would do well to remember that."

"I think it does."

"You see, if I'm in a clown outfit, your perception of me is different than when I was in rags, is it not?"

"Yes."

"A clown can make people laugh and a merry heart doeth good like a medicine."

"Where have I heard that before?"

"You'll find it in the Bible. So many people are sick in this world, suffering from some dreadful disease or other. How much better would they feel if a clown entered the room and made them laugh?"

"There's no laughter in a hospital bed."

"You're right about that. If you can make someone laugh, Katie, you have done more in those moments than some people ever do in a lifetime. The gift of making people laugh can be a calling."

"I never thought about it like that."

"No, I don't imagine you did," he said with a smile that lit up those blue eyes. "Did you bring the hammer and the chisel?"

"I knew you would ask me that," I said, pulling them out of my backpack. "Here," I said handing them to him.

"Oh no. I don't want them."

"Well, what do you want me to do with them?"

"Did they teach you anything?"

"Were they supposed to?"

"Yes, they were supposed to."

"Okay."

"Well?"

"All I could think about is that my father used a hammer and a chisel most every time he built something."

"That's true. He did. A hammer and a chisel represent a man's hard work, especially a man who works with his hands like your father did, but there's more."

"There is?"

"Yes. Don't you see? It's like I started to tell you before. A hammer can build something or it can tear it down. A chisel can go into some pretty tough places and it can do the same thing. However, you see, Katie, your words are like a hammer. They can tear down a person or they can build them up. A hammer drives a nail into the wood and your words can often drive a message into someone's heart."

"You offer a different perspective on everything," I said with another smile.

"It's one of the things I do best. A hammer and a chisel build a foundation and what your foundation is built on makes a huge difference when the storms of life come—and as I told you before, they will always come, Katie, as long as there is life, the storms will come."

"I've already been through too many storms," I noted with the sadness that seemed to wrap itself around my already heavy heart. My heart was always heavy from carrying those burdens like I packed them up in a suitcase and carried them with me where ever I went.

"I've told you, Katie, the burdens were never yours to carry. When you release a burden, then you can see the answer. And back to the foundation. What you build your life on matters. The hammer and the chisel can build a house that can't be torn down but it's built with the things that matter—those things that people can't tear down."

"I get it."

"I hope so. A foundation that is built on truth, and the unshakeable truth of who you are as a person is one that a storm from hell will not be able to tear down. The foundation is your life, Katie. What your life is built on will matter when the storm comes. It's what you believe and stand for *before* the storm that determines the outcome *after* the storm."

"I wish I hadn't been through so many storms in my life."

"Storms can be your teachers if you let them. If you believe in the One who made you then no storm will ever be able to destroy you, no matter how fierce its winds and regardless of how high the water rises."

"I've never thought of it like that."

"Didn't think so."

"What in the world am I supposed to do with a hammer and a chisel?"

"Think about something else when you look at them. Let the hammer drive away all the unforgiveness that's been building up inside of you for much of your life."

"How did you know that?" I whispered.

"It's true isn't it?"

"Yes." That was about all I could manage to say.

"Why don't you forgive all those who didn't know who you really are? They're the ones with the real problem, not you. If they don't see you for who you are and what your life represents, it's not your fault. Forgiveness is a choice, Katie."

"It's really hard to let it go."

"I know but like I said, you can't go forward if you're always looking back."

"What have I gotten myself into," I said with a laugh.

"You mean all because you took five dollars from a homeless man?"

"I guess so. But some how I don't think you're homeless, are you?"

"I might be, but then again I might not be." *Those eyes and that radiance of light around him!* Who *was* he?

"It bears repeating, Katie but people judge what they do not know and they condemn what they do not understand. There is always more to the story than the one you write."

"So, okay, what am I supposed to do with the hammer and chisel," I persisted.

"They're like a lot of things in life, Katie. If you don't use that hammer and chisel, and all you do is stare at them, they don't serve a purpose except to lay around unused. A chisel refines things and gets into some really tough places. Just keep the hammer and chisel somewhere that makes you look at them every day. Think about how you want to build with your life. What do you want your message to be?"

"I don't know but I promise I will think about how I want to build my life."

"Let me know next time if they taught you anything. Spend some serious time with just you and that hammer and chisel."

With that message, he got up off the bench, did what I call a little Red Skeleton hop, tweaked his clown nose that he'd put back on, waved and around the corner he went.

Maybe one day soon I would know his real identity. For now, I packed up the hammer and chisel and went home, setting them up against the fireplace in my living room.

Staring at them might teach me something and on the third day, the light went on in my heart. They taught me something! I couldn't wait to tell him.

Chapter Seven

Okay, where was he? I had waited for two hours, and he wasn't here!

Oh no! I prayed something didn't happen to him.

Where could he be?

I was just about to get up off the bench and leave when he rounded the corner, waved at me from beneath his tattered hat as he walked toward me.

"You're late!" I said impulsively.

"Sometimes there are things that detain me, Katie. Like an assignment—that sort of thing," he added mysteriously.

"Are you an undercover narc visiting me at a park bench?" I asked with a laugh. Somehow, I doubted that.

"No. However, I do occasionally have other business to tend to, as the saying goes."

Something made me look at his hands and when I did what I saw startled me and I gasped.

"Your hands!"

"I wondered when you would notice," he said gently.

"You're not going to tell me now if I ask you, are you?"

"No, Katie. Not now. So back to that hammer and chisel."

"I stared at them and suddenly, something occurred to me. My father always said that a hammer could build a bridge, and a chisel could make sure that bridge would never fall apart, that is if you built it right. We need to build bridges in this world."

"How so?"

"There's so much hatred, what I call *strife and debate* in this world. We need to build bridges that forge a new path, one that builds peace and reconciliation instead of hatred and division."

"That's a mighty profound insight, Katie and it's a good one. A hammer and a chisel in the hands of someone who doesn't know how to use them is meaningless because if a person doesn't know how to use them, all they do is just put them aside, store them somewhere and forget about them. They don't use them for their designated purpose."

"No, they don't."

"The gifts you're given in this life are like that. If you "store up" the gifts and never use them, they won't do anyone much good. It's like keeping those gifts hidden in a drawer and you never take them out to use them so they just sit there."

"I wish I knew what my gifts are, I mean I know some of them but not all of them."

"We are all given gifts—some tangible and some intangible. The question is: What do you do with them?"

"I don't know exactly."

"It's like this, Katie. Let's suppose I give you a gift card for a hundred dollars. You stick it in your wallet – just like those five dollars I gave you – but let's say you need groceries. You were given one hundred dollars in a gift card, but you refuse to use it. It was given to you as a gift, but you refused to use it and the gift was there, but because you refused to use it, you still needed groceries. It wasn't because you didn't receive the gift to buy those groceries. Life is like that. So are the gifts you're given. If you don't use them, no one receives the benefits from them and neither do you. The gift of making people laugh is an intangible gift but let's say you don't ever use it to make someone else laugh. People will miss a lot of joy and healing because you refused to use the gift of laughter."

"I'd be pretty selfish if I didn't use my gifts to help someone else."

"That would be true. Now give me your hand."

"Why?"

"You ask too many questions. Just give me your hand."

I did.

I had never felt such warmth flow into my hand in my entire life. "You're staring at my hands," he said gently.

"Yes, I am," I admitted but I knew I couldn't ask him about his hands because he wouldn't tell me.

"Now," he said, "close your hand into a fist."

I did.

"So your hand is closed into a fist. Can you get anything into your hand?"

"No. Nothing," I said.

"Now open your hand."

I did.

"With your hand wide open, your palms are turned to the sky. It causes you to look up, Katie. With your hand open, your palms are pointed to something greater than you and you can receive because your hand is open. You will never receive anything if your hand is always clenched tight, closed and in a fist. However, if your hand is open, you can receive anything into your hand."

"Oh my. I never thought of that." Then came the tears that opened like a floodgate and poured down my face.

"Too many people in your life have lived with a clenched fist. That's not your fault. You were taught to give and few people follow that example. Giving is the answer to opening the secret places."

"The secret places?"

"Sometimes in life there seems to be no answer, no solution. Giving brings you into the secret place."

"What is the secret place—*where* is it?"

"The secret place is found when you help those who are poor, someone who cries out for help and cannot help themselves. It opens up the reservoirs of heaven—those secret places in heaven that you cannot see—and then it has sort of a ripple effect, causing those reservoirs to open and pour out the blessings in miraculous ways. Sometimes a miracle is the only thing that will do. Do you believe in miracles, Katie?"

"I do. I need a whole bunch of them. Sometimes I don't think I will ever figure out my life and get out of what seems to be a never-ending vicious cycle."

"Go back to that five-dollar bill. What you give away is often more important than what you keep. That five dollars was just five dollars until you gave it away. Life is about more than money. It takes only your time to make a phone call to someone who is lonely or sick, who needs to hear a kind voice, someone to encourage them. It only takes a moment to thank someone or put into force what the world refers to as a *random act of kindness*. Nothing is ever random in this life, neither is there any such thing as coincidence."

"The world believes in coincidence."

"Yes, but I do not. Always remember this: *there is no such thing as coincidence but rather those were the times when God chooses to remain anonymous.*"

"Mama believed there was a reason for everything."

"Everything does happen for a reason, Katie and nothing catches God by surprise. God sees everything and He knows what will happen before it does."

"Now, here," he said. He pushed something into my hands. It was, of all things, a rope.

"What in God's name, no pun intended, do you want me to do with this rope?"

"For now, take it home with you. Next Sunday bring it back to the bench with you and bring a box of matches with you."

"A box of matches?"

"You're not hard of hearing," he said with a laugh. "You heard that correctly. A box of matches."

He left on the opposite side of the park today, and when he turned, a shimmer of something emitted from his hand as he threw it up in a wave.

Five dollars from a homeless man and now I was going home with a rope.

His words echoed in my ears. *There is no such thing as coincidence.*

Chapter Eight

I stared at that rope all week long when I came in from work and before I went to sleep and before I went to work.

For a reason I didn't understand that rope bothered me, but I had no idea why.

After all, it was just a rope. Somehow, though, I knew it really *wasn't* just a rope.

I looked forward to Sundays on the bench in the park. I didn't know who he really was and doubtless, he wasn't just a homeless man, but perhaps one day he would tell me his real identity.

He was dressed in overalls today. He made me smile. I had come to understand he never looked the same on any given Sunday.

"Why the overalls?"

"I look kind of dapper in them, don't you think?"

"You do."

"Overalls. What do they make you think of?"

"A farmer. Daddy always wore overalls."

"It's that thing again, Katie. You know about how people perceive others by what they see. Did you bring the rope?"

"It's right here," I said pulling it out of my backpack.

"Did you bring the matches?"

"Yep, got them, too," I continued as I pulled them from my backpack.

"Okay, good girl!" He said with a smile. "Now hand me the rope and the matches."

"Is this how to burn a rope 101?" I asked with a laugh as I handed him the rope and the matches.

He took them from my hands and placed the rope in his lap, alongside the matches. "Did the rope teach you anything?"

"For the life of me, no."

"It should have. You see, as much as a rope can secure something, what it secures is not always good. A rope symbolizes bondage, holding onto something or a rope attaches itself to something—or someone—in a way that hurts them."

"Wouldn't you know I never thought about it like that?"

"I didn't think you did," he replied with that familiar laugh.

"I catch on pretty quick most of the time. I promise."

"I think you do," he said, laughing again. "Now listen. As long as you hold onto this rope it can tie you to something good or it can tie you to something bad—in essence it can be a symbol of good or bad. When you pray for someone and it doesn't look like anything is changing, what you're doing is holding the rope for them."

"Oh my God," I said, "I never thought about that."

"Sometimes the rope you hold for someone else is the only lifeline they have. You have to ask yourself the question *if you don't hold the rope for them, who will?*"

"That's pretty true."

"I always speak the truth."

"I'm sure you do," I said, laughing again.

"A rope can symbolize many things—you hold onto a rope that ties you to your past or you hold onto a rope that ties you to a hurt or a devastation. And sometimes a rope binds you to things and people that are not good for you."

"So I need to let the rope go," I asked softly.

"This is what you need to learn," he replied. He took the rope and held it in his hands and then he lit a match and set the rope on fire, being careful to watch it catch the flames closely to him so he could put it out. "Now, here's the lesson and don't ever forget it, Katie. *The only things you lose when you go through the fire are the things that bound you.*"

"Oh."

"You have been bound long enough and sometimes you have to let it go. That's often what happens when you walk through the fire – when things are hard and there seems to be no answers. That fire is trying to get you to let go of your past, of the wounds and the scars that never quite healed. And you, Katie, have been needing to heal for a long time now."

There were those tears again! He very quietly watched me weep without a word and the only thing he did was take his hand and cover mine. "You never really walk alone, Katie. Don't you know that?"

"I do now."

"You have never been alone even in the darkest of times. In those moments when you thought all hope was lost, or the storm would never end, you have not been alone."

"Will you always show up on this bench?"

"I will be here for a while, Katie."

I looked at what remained of the rope, which wasn't much, just a few fibers.

He handed me the matches and the remnants from the rope. "Keep this remnant as a reminder of what I said. Remnants are those things that are symbols of the past that no longer is."

"Thank you."

"For what?"

"I don't know who you are, and I don't know if you will ever tell me, but thank you. You are touching my heart and changing my life."

"It's what I do," he replied as he tipped his tattered hat, got up once again from the bench and meandered across the park, this time stopping to pick up what looked like pieces of trash scattered in various places. He put them in the pocket of his overalls and once again disappeared. This time he didn't turn back to wave. He just vanished.

I sat on the bench for a while this time. Usually, I left right after he did but not so today. It was such a beautiful day, one of those days when the sky was so blue you could almost touch it, there was a chill in the air, the first signs of winter setting in. The cool wind on my face was refreshing, but yet it was more than that!

"Dear God," I said from my place on the bench, "I don't know if you can hear me or not, but I think you can. Thank you for sending whoever it is you must surely have sent to me. I've been searching for a long time. Amen."

I got up and went home. For the first time I didn't feel lonely as I had felt for such a long time now. There was something different now and I realized what it was.

I had been beaten down by life's circumstances for a long time now, caught up in the tailspin of adversity, wondering if my life would ever change, searching for answers that I never thought would come. However, now something felt different.

The wind changed.

And for the first time that I could ever remember, I knew what the difference was.

I had found hope.

Chapter Nine

He was on the bench this time before I got there. Today he was dressed in a white suit, kind of odd for this time of year but I had learned with my friend that there was always a message or a reason for the way he dressed.

"What's with the white suit?" I asked.

"I see you noticed," he replied with that smile.

"You can't miss it. It's so beautiful. And the blue shirt, kinda nice, too."

"Thank you. White is one of my favorite colors. I won't be coming here much longer, Katie."

"You won't?" I said, afraid to let the tears show but somehow a tear slid down my face anyway.

"No."

"Why?"

"There are certain things I must say to you and when that is finished, I have to leave."

"Will you tell me who you are before you go?"

"Yes, I will. I promise."

"You have made me find hope just when I thought all hope was lost."

"There are things I must say to you now, Katie. First of all, there is always hope. Every person on earth has hope. They only have to look for it and it will be there."

"I know that now."

"Hope is eternal, that wellspring that rises up inside your spirit. Hope is for all people. You have hope and a purpose and the two are twin companions, so to speak."

I kept staring at his hands. "Will you tell me about your hands before you go?"

"I will. You have felt lost for a very long time now, Katie, but here is something else I want you to always remember: *You may have been lost but you were never lost to God.*"

He took both of my hands into his and held them, looking at me as he did so. "There is much I must tell you and you must never forget it."

"I'm listening." And I meant it.

"Katie, the world seems at peril so much of the time with growing divisions, hatred and unrest but the world is not at war with people so much as it is at war with itself. We war with what we do not understand and what we do not know—much like what I told you before about judgment and condemnation. Do you know what your purpose is yet, Katie?"

"No, but I will find it, of that I'm sure."

"You have already found it you just don't realize it."

"Maybe so."

"I know so. Now listen," he said earnestly, holding my hands a bit tighter. "There are things you must know. A man will win a war on his knees and not in the boardroom. The battles are always with the things we do not understand. Wars and battles come from within the mind when seeds of hatred, envy, bitterness, strife, jealousy, and rage are planted in the mind. Every seed bears fruit of its own kind. You know, like the way your father planted seed for his crops as a farmer."

"It all makes sense now. Why are you dressed in white," I blurted out before I had time to think about it.

"White is a symbol of light and the world needs light now more than ever. There is always light in the darkness."

THE MAN ON THE BENCH

"And I suppose you won't tell me why you're dressed in white—at least not yet?"

He smiled, "You catch on pretty quick."

"Sometimes I think I'm a little slow on the uptake."

"No, I don't think so," he said softly. He reached behind him and pulled out something that looked like a pipe.

"What in the world is that?"

"Some people call it a pipe. I like to think of it as a plumbline." He lifted it above his head and stretched out his arms until it ran "arm-to-arm".

"Why did you do that?"

"You see, Katie Ellen, when the plumbline is stretched straight out, it frees the flow of whatever needs to come through it to reach its destination. However, if it's bent or clogged up, nothing can get through or at the very least, it makes it almost impossible for it to get through."

"And the message is," I asked softly, knowing there was going to be one.

"When people pray for help, often the *plumbline* is clogged up because they have held onto bitterness, anger, resentment or unforgiveness. It clogs it up so your prayer gets stuck inside the plumbline somewhere between when you issued the prayer and when you were trying to get it to the other side."

"I will never look at plumbing the same way ever again."

"No," he said with a laugh, "I don't think you will. A plumbline is like a phone line in many respects, or better yet, think of it like this—it's your pipeline to God."

"Well, there you have it. I think my plumbline must have been clogged up for years."

"No, not always. God hears every prayer but there are evil forces also that try to stop those prayers from getting through. Here, let me show you something," he said. He reached down on the other side of the bench and in his hands, he held rocks and pieces of gravel. "See this?" he said, "Now look." He stuck them inside the plumbline as he called it. Then he reached over and picked up a bottle of water and tried to pour it into the plumbline from the other end. It couldn't get through! "The water couldn't get through because the rocks and pieces of gravel stood in the way. So, always remember that, as the old saying goes, *there are two sides to every coin.* Your prayers can be hindered or blocked because of the things in your heart that aren't right, like unforgiveness, anger, resentment, even envy and jealousy—OR they can be blocked because an evil force between heaven and earth tries to stop it—thus, the rocks and gravel."

"You are a genius!" I exclaimed with a laugh. "Absolute pure genius!"

"No, I don't think that. It's just a rule of spiritual law."

"You're going to leave, aren't you?" I said suddenly, sadness welling up inside of me.

"Yes," he said softly. "I will leave soon. When my purpose is finished."

"Your purpose? What is your purpose?"

He smiled and didn't say a word.

"Okay, you're probably going to tell me that when I'm supposed to know what your purpose is, you'll tell me."

"Good girl!" He laughed again then the expression on his face turned somber. "I must leave but come again next Sunday." He turned to go.

"What about the plumbline?" I said, noticing he left it on the bench.

"It will always be there," he said as he rounded the corner, a shimmer of white from his suit casting light against the sky.

"Next Sunday," I yelled after him.

He turned and waved, saying something I couldn't understand because it sounded like his words were caught up in the wind. And like so many other times, he was gone.

I went home to my small apartment and what had seemed to be my rather meaningless life and I got out the watch, the chisel and hammer, the pack of seeds and stared at all of them. Somewhere inside each of them were profound lessons I somehow needed to learn.

I realized I had no money on me and that I needed to go to the nearest ATM to get money before the week started, so I grabbed my purse and headed out the door.

When I got to the ATM, I opened my wallet and stared at what was inside.

A five-dollar bill. *How in the world?*

I got money from the ATM careful to tuck the five-dollar bill in a different compartment.

Five dollars from a homeless man had changed my life forever. Little did I know.

Chapter Ten

The next Sunday I arrived at the bench earlier than usual, a sense of wonder and anticipation in my heart, like a light shining inside of me. I couldn't explain it even if I had wanted to.

Two hours later I was still waiting and as I did, I began to weep, the tears flowing like a freefall down my face. *I've lost him!* It was the only thought in my head and it was truly what I felt!

I pulled the watch out of my purse and set it on the bench, then I pulled out the pack of seeds and then the hammer and the chisel, staring at things unexplainable as I took the five dollars out of my wallet.

Five dollars from a homeless man.

When I turned around on the bench I noticed an envelope and the handwriting simply said: "*Five Dollars from a Homeless Man*".

I opened it and inside was a letter from my friend. This is what he wrote:

THE LETTER

My lovely Katie Ellen,

I know you were expecting me to be at the bench today and I am, in a way. I'm really here with you! I promise!

Remember I told you there wasn't much time and that I wouldn't be with you much longer?

THE MAN ON THE BENCH

The time has come for me to leave you but there are things that I must now tell you. I knew you would bring the watch, the pack of seeds, and the hammer and the chisel.

You have walked many miles in your young life, always seeking but thinking that you would never find. Your shoes have held you hostage to your past as you always kept one foot in the past and the other pointed towards an uncertain future. And you were always wearing shoes that no longer fit.

Nothing is ever uncertain with God, Katie Ellen. Remember that. Like the rope we burned, sometimes you have to remember that you can never go forward if you're always looking back. I told you that.

I came to you for a season and for a purpose. Am I really homeless? No.

I came disguised as a common man, a homeless man who had spent his life living inside cardboard boxes and under bridges.

Why?

Because the homeless man, just like the poor, the sick, the old and the dying are often thrown away, tossed into the sewer of life like a piece of trash, forgotten because so many people believe their lives don't matter.

They do.

Perception is how the world generates its view of people—like the tattered clothes of a homeless man, the overalls of a farmer or the six-hundred-dollar suit and the jewels of the rich man—they all come with a perception one way or the other.

Disguises can be deceiving and certainly people are not always who they seem to be.

We met because I sat in my rags on a park bench and because the destiny and lesson of a five-dollar bill was as I tried to teach you, greater than the sum total of its parts.

This is not Lessons 101, Katie but here is another lesson for you. If you cry out to God because you need $100,000 to get out of a mess and you meet a total stranger in a store and feel compelled to tell him your story and your need. If that man is a millionaire and you don't know it, when he returns home if God commands him to give you the $100,000 then you just got your miracle, and that man will receive a hundredfold in this lifetime and eternal life because he helped someone in need.

However, if that man ignored the cry of your heart and the command from God then God must seek a willing heart to answer your cry for a miracle.

Miracles do exist, Katie. It's those things you can't explain because if you could explain it, then it wouldn't be a miracle.

When you were a little girl, about nine years old, you told God something you wanted to do one day. You told Him you thought that's what you were supposed to do. Now here you are all those years later and yet, that dream has not come to pass.

God heard the cries of a little girl all those years ago just like he saw your tears at the bedside of your dying mother as she was being lifted into the arms of the angels.

He has always embraced you silently when your pillows were stained with the tears you thought no one ever saw.

Never forget these things, Katie. Five dollars is just five dollars until you meet the need of someone who has nothing. The seeds you plant not only change your life but they often change the lives of those you touch. For instance, about those tomato seeds. If you planted a bumper crop of tomatoes and people near you were hungry, those tomatoes just fed a family because you took the harvest from your seed and shared it with someone who needed food. Remember that.

The hammer and the chisel create and destroy, build up and tear down. A foundation that is built on the rock of what is right will never be shaken even in the most terrible of storms. You can build a bridge or you can tear it down—the choice is in your hands, much like that chisel and hammer. It's what you do with them that makes all the difference in the world.

Our words define us in so many ways. When we use our words to tear down someone else, we often destroy a precious part of that person's soul.

When we build our lives around the things that matter—those simple acts can change the world, Katie Ellen.

Build your life around love and acts of magnanimous generosity. Make your life about giving. In other words, "give to live and live to give."

Forge new paths by daring to be who God created you to be and make no apologies for who—and what you are—because you are created in His own image.

Your value is in God, not the world's opinions of who and what you should be.

It is never too late to start over, to plant seeds of forgiveness. Forgiveness starts with you.

Forgive yourself. When you do that, you can give forgiveness to others.

Remember I told you that forgiveness is a choice. It is often hard to forgive an enemy, especially one who has been cruel but in the giving of forgiveness it sets you free and you are no longer held hostage by the damage done to you.

The world is in peril these days in so many ways. As you look around the world in which you live, you do not have to look very far to see the hatred and the bitterness that seems to be embracing the world at every turn.

Hatred, as I said before, is a seed that begins in the mind. Once planted it moves into thoughts and thoughts become actions.

Love is all that really matters.

We must love those who are different from us, love those who do not agree with us or believe as we do. Love cancels all debts, Katie Ellen. Don't ever forget that.

Mercy is always to be freely given because if a man will not give mercy, how can he one day expect to receive mercy himself?

There is no victory in hatred, no solace or comfort in hatred. The bottom line is simply this: We are all God's people.

What is your purpose? When you were nine years old you told God you thought you could change the world with your pen.

You have not picked up your pen in seven years. Why? Because you were afraid. Remember the plumbline, Katie Ellen?

Sometimes we travel a crooked road thinking we will never reach our final destination, our place of purpose and our destiny but often it is the crooked road that leads us to our greater lessons because that crooked road was our teacher. The crooked road is often where the miracles lie.

God gave you a gift and often you never knew the stories that needed to be written. Write the stories of all the nameless faces, the forgotten ones—the people who have no voice. YOU are their voice.

With your pen and your voice—and all the good that will emerge from them your other purpose is to help the poor, to help those who have nothing.

Everyone has a story, Katie Ellen, both the stories you see with the natural eye and the hidden layers beneath the story.

God cares about the homeless man living under the bridge and in cardboard boxes, ransacking garbage dumps for food. He cares about the children crying for food because there is none. He cares about the family that can't pay their mortgage and keep a roof over their head. He cares about the common man—the man who often feels abandoned by the world.

God cares about the elderly, those people like your parents who didn't do anything wrong: "They just got old." If people live long enough, they will get old.

Tell this message to the world, Katie Ellen. Tell them one simple truth: God loves them. Tell them how much he loves them. He loves them just as they are, with all their flaws and imperfections and human frailties.

Help them understand that love is what will erase the hatred in this world and stop the wars—both the wars on the battlefields and the wars within the soul. As I told you before, there are the wars you see and the ones you can't see.

God loves every person no matter who they are or where they come from. He loves all people regardless of race or nationality or anything else for that matter.

You asked who I am, Katie Ellen. Don't you know? As a little girl crying out to God you asked Him for one thing. Now, all these years later after enormous adversity, unrelenting grief and a life that seems as if it's going nowhere, one night in your apartment do you remember what you did?

You got down on your knees and said, "God if you are real, show me who You are. Come and find me. Help me find my way."

God loves people so much that He sent me. *I know a great deal about mercy and forgiveness because of what you saw on my hands.*

Those were scars from the nails driven into my hands and those same scars are in my feet.

Some do not believe that I exist, Katie Ellen. Many people deny Me. But I am He. The Risen Christ.

I loved a young woman, you, so much that I came to you with five dollars from a homeless man.

I have come before, and I will come again. Tell my people that I love them.

Look at your watch, Katie Ellen. A watch signifies time. Time is precious, a fragile commodity. Tell my people to spend their time loving one another, giving mercy and forgiveness. Tell them that love will stop the hate.

When the time on that watch moves, once the time is gone you can never get it back again. It moves forward and no man can control time.

Your time is precious and so is the time of others. Tell them, Katie, will you do that for me?

That is your purpose. Tell the world who I really am. Tell them that I love them with everything in the wounds I suffered for them. Tell them one more time that I have come before, and I will come again.

Keep the watch with you always as a reminder that yesterday is a cancelled check, tomorrow is a promissory note and today is cash in hand.

Lives depend on what you tell them, Katie Ellen. Pick up your pen. Write the story. Tell them about *Five Dollars from a Homeless Man*.

Tell them to help the poor and those who have nothing, to give love and mercy to all people. Tell them that the way to blessing is to give to the poor and help those who have nothing. Remember, Katie Ellen. *A faithful man shall abound with blessing.*

Tell them for me, will you? Tell the story of our Sundays on the bench.

You will meet with resistance from some but press in and never veer from the message. Tell my people that I love them.

Tell them I love them more than they may know or understand but I love them, the poor, the hungry, the rich, the homeless, the young, the old, the dying and all those people who think they are lost.

Tell them what I told you: They have been lost but they were never lost to God.

You want to know if you will see me again, Katie Ellen.

Yes, you will see me time and again to uplift your purpose and to help you but remember this: it may not be as a homeless man.

You will live a life of purpose and with hope that springs eternal. If you need help, just ask. God heard you the first time and I assure you He will hear you the next time.

I love you, Katie Ellen Winthrop. I love all people. Tell them that. Tell them I love them. I can't emphasize it enough.

I am only a breath away, Katie Ellen. If you need me, whisper my name. I can fly faster than you can fall. Never forget that.

This is your purpose. Tell my people how much I love them.

Until we meet again—here's another five dollars from a homeless man.

You know what to do with it.

I stared at the words written on the pages of his letter, tears streaming down my face, knowing with certainty that He spoke the truth.

I picked up the letter, tucked it inside the envelope, put the five dollars in my wallet and pressed the letter next to my heart and when I did I felt a prick. I took the letter away and noticed a tiny drop of blood.

I heard the sounds of wind, a still small voice almost like a rushing wind in the breeze and I looked toward the sky.

White light shot across the sky, the wind blowing against my face. I knew with unfailing certainty that I had met The Shepherd.

Some people may not believe my story but that didn't matter. I had to tell my story. And I would tell it as many times as it needed to be told.

I turned to go, wiping the tears from my face and on the way out of the park, there was a homeless man, this one curled up inside a cardboard box.

He looked at me with sad eyes, eyes filled with hopelessness, weary I am sure of the journey, feeling lost as though no one cared about him.

I reached down and touched his face, dirty I'm sure from being unable to take a bath.

I said softly: "He loves you. He has come before and He will come again."

Then I pressed a five-dollar bill into his hand.

Five Dollars from a Homeless Man.

The man on the bench.

I looked up into the sky and could not stop crying as I whispered, "Thank you for loving me so much that you came to my rescue. I will not fail you. And I will keep this promise forever. I love you."

I walked out of the park, went home and picked up my pen near my nightstand. On the night stand I wasn't surprised to find it again. *Five dollars from a homeless man.*

The man on the bench.

MY STORY

I have always thought it important to be transparent with my readers and this time is no different. In fact, it's far more important with this book because of the scope and the power of its message. Having said that, I'm not sure my readers can understand why I wrote this book without telling "my story behind the story".

Quite a long time ago, God spoke to my heart and told me to write a book that tells people who He really is.

Sometimes we search for Jesus and think He isn't real because we can't seem to find Him in the church pews, the hallelujah choruses or anywhere else, for that matter. Oftentimes we find ourselves asking questions for which there seem to be no answers.

I have known the real Jesus for a very long time but for quite a few years it seemed I was catapulted into one life event after the other, all coupled with enormous adversity in one form or another.

I took care of my beloved mother for ten and a half years until she became critically ill, and I had to authorize physicians to remove her from lifer support. It was the most devastating moments of my life. After her passing, I met with a lot of trouble from family over my mother's estate and as a result I suffered enormous setbacks and losses for which there seemed to be no recovery.

I cried out to God for help and kept crying and crying, every day, for a miracle, for a road out of the mess my life had become through no fault of my own.

I remember one time when there was no food in the house, and I had to pray for God to send food—He did. He sent it through a person, not a church.

I remember thinking, where was the church?

For the life of me, I could not tell you. They were nowhere to be found.

Then there were the massive repairs to the house I lived in—built by my father. I remember calling worldwide ministries and churches, both local and national, asking for help, explaining how long my mother had been sick and that I could not work, etc. The standard answers were almost identical, "We only do disaster relief, ma'am."

I remember screaming into the phone. "This IS a disaster. It's a silent disaster that's happening to thousands if not millions of people."

It was a response that fell on deaf ears, and then it was the first time I asked the question to the Lord: "What do you do when the church don't come?"

One of my losses was my transportation and because of the loss, I wound up riding a public transport for a very long time.

What does that have to do with my journey and my story?

Absolutely everything!

You see, all those years I spent listening to sermons, knowing Jesus up close and personal, singing the hymns, and praising Jesus in the pews could not have prepared me for the extraordinary journey on the road up ahead.

While riding on that transport, God transformed my life as I began to seek Him in a different way.

Why? I met so many people on the transport whose only help was that transport. I met people who changed my life—and my heart—forever—one person at a time.

Their stories, their struggles and their own hardships and adversities often paled in comparison to mine and so touched my heart in such a profound way that I could not possibly be the same ever again.

When we look beyond our own circumstances and begin to see people through God's eyes, life does indeed begin to change.

This particular Christmas, I was still without a car, and I asked a neighbor to take me to two people's residences so I could bring them Christmas gifts even though they did not know me. The first stop was at the home of a man who had been on dialysis for almost ten years and up and down out of a wheelchair. The second stop was to give Christmas to the wife of another man who rode the shuttle. She was his caregiver as he fought kidney failure, life in a wheelchair and other maladies, as well as frequent visits to the local emergency room, many of which resulted in lengthy hospital stays.

The neighbor who took me to their homes said to me in a quizzical way. "You have empathy. You need help and yet you're out here giving to these people."

I responded in kind. "Yes, I have been in trouble for a long time, but this man is sick, and this woman is a forgotten caregiver to her husband. There are people in this world you can find who are far more worse off than you."

The results of those two Christmas visits were some of my many blessings.

The man in that wheelchair for almost ten years, on dialysis three times a week with other health complications became one of my dearest friends. His name was Lonnie. His humor amidst the storms of life often brought me to tears. His sons abandoned him and a woman who was his friend became his caregiver. He walked he earth for many years as a crippled man, but a stronger, kinder man I have never met. When we first became friends, he looked at me one day at the local McDonald's where we stopped on the way to a medical appointment. "How long you been without a car?"

At that time the answer was, "Two and a half years."

After a hospital stay, he let me use his truck to go pick up a few things for him. When I returned with his items and turned to leave, he stood a little wobbly by the sofa, balancing himself with his cane when he said, "Wait just a minute." Then he pulled out his wallet and handed me money, saying as he did so, "You've been in trouble a long time and you've been praying for help for a long time." Those words profoundly touched my heart and brought me to tears.

The Lord used a crippled man to help me.

On the day he died, it was one of the saddest days of my life and since his passing, I have often asked this question about him—as I have so many others, **"Lord, what happens to the Lonnie's of the world?"**

The woman who was the caregiver for her husband also became a dear friend and we traveled a road of love and support, often praying for her husband, Larry, as he endured many medical complications.

That transport became God's way of showing me His truth—and the needs of so many lost people.

And that transport saved my life!

I went in search of groceries and a way to get from "A to B" and behind the cloak of a public transport and a "big white bus" as I learned to call it, God began to show me His face and who He really is.

I took that transport to a local chapel and sat, staring up at the Crucifixion, light streaming in through the stained-glass windows as tears streamed down my face. That's the day He said, "Write a book that tells people who I really am."

You are holding that book in your hands.

There were many times during those 7 ½ years (yes, 7 ½ years) that I felt abandoned, betrayed, lonely, forsaken and yes, "thrown away". I knew that the real Jesus was the one who showed up in a big white bus on a public transport with drivers behind the wheel who were the hands and hearts of Jesus.

I knew the real Jesus was the one in the food bank lines and the One that brought the food to my front porch when I had no way to get it. He is the face of every homeless person in a cardboard box or under a bridge. He is the One with His hand and tears upon the person in a wheelchair on dialysis, whose life is about one medical emergency after the other.

He brought "angels unaware" to cut the grass or jump the fence to "donate" fixing an electrical issue. He was the face of kindness in a stranger who offered help when those who knew me would not.

The church itself did not come during my journey. Phone calls to churches were, for the most part, unanswered, or I was simply turned away. I remember one time calling a local church about their food bank when they asked where I lived. When I told them they said, "It was outside their borders." My response was that Jesus did not have borders.

When someone cries out to God with tears streaming down their face, He hears those liquid prayers.

I asked Him what He wanted to me to say to the world at large on His behalf and His message is contained inside this book.

And this is what I would like to tell you. The Jesus that I know loves you.

He loves you and He loves all people. He said, "Tell my people I love them."

There are many people throughout the world who do not understand His Cross and the

Act of Mercy when He was on that Cross.

He came so that all people might have life and have it more abundantly. His death served as a reminder to all of us of His Divine Mercy.

How so? First of all, as The Christ He could have stopped His Crucifixion but as He said after forty days in the wilderness, "Not my will but thine."

Alongside His Cross there were thieves on the Cross and one of them simply told Him he was a thief and asked for forgiveness. He gave it.

He gave forgiveness and mercy to all those who beat Him and put Him on that Cross.

Divine Mercy means His mercy endureth forever. It is perfect Mercy washed in His blood and offered to all who will receive it.

His Divine Mercy is about forgiveness, about caring enough for the world that He would die on a Cross and rise again on the third day to show the world not only that He is the savior but that in the Resurrection there is no death.

Wherever you are in your life as you read this book—He loves you. He loves the drug addict, the alcoholic, the homeless, the one addicted to porn, the one walking outside His laws. He does NOT judge anyone. He simply loves you. As you are.

He can take a broken heart, a broken life and the broken pieces of shattered dreams and put it back together better than any of us could.

I am so thankful for His Divine Mercy that He gave to me and for the beautiful way in which He carried me when I could not carry myself.

He was with me before the storm, in the storm and after the storm.

I often say to Him, "I ain't never seen you but if people knew you how could they not love you?"

His Cross is about His love for all people, His Divine Mercy and though it isn't often preached, it is also about His Mother who wept at the foot of the Cross when he lay dying on the Cross, but she is also the one who rejoiced three days later when the stone was lifted away and He walked from the tomb.

If you will let Him, He will wrap His arms around you and simply love you. He does, you know, love you. Yes, you! He loves you no matter what.

Always remember this: "You may have been lost but you were never lost to God. You never really walk alone. The ONLY things you lose when you go through the fire are the things that bound you." And finally, "There is no such thing as coincidence but rather

those were the times when God chose to remain anonymous."

He is always with you.

During the journey that led me to write this book, my life was intertwined with a homeless man who became my friend, and his story is one that deserves to be weaved inside this book. I believe his life and his story will capture your heart forever.

JERRY'S STORY

If you notice at the beginning of this book, it is dedicated to two people, the last of which is to Jerry Sanders (August 2nd, 1965 – August 15th, 2024).

There's a reason for that.

Jerry and I became friends in an odd sort of way, depending on your perspective given this world of ever-changing digital technology.

He and I were both on a business platform that focused on film and the creative arts. I joined as a writer, and he joined as someone interested in one day working in film and being a film producer. That was his first love when it came to his dreams of success. It was what ignited a passion in his heart. On that platform one day, he showed up asking to connect so I responded with a "yes."

He asked if he could call and talk about writing and film and again, I said, "Yes."

I joined that platform in hopes of resurrecting my very broken career because I'd been away from writing for more than a decade to take care of my beloved mother—and it was also during the beginning of "those seven unforgettable years".

When he called, we talked for a long time about absolutely nothing personal and only about film and my writing – the previous books I'd published and his love of film.

Shortly thereafter I put up a GoFundMe campaign because I was pretty desperate for help with repairs on the house my father built (the one I inherited; built in 1960 with so many looming, major repairs).

Jerry responded in such a kind, beautiful way simply by donating every two weeks on his payday from his "day" job in the financial markets.

Then he would call, and we'd talk about his family and the ups and downs of his life—and always, I would thank him for his generosity, which in turn, enabled me to actually have some important repairs done.

On another day he called and said, "You know you're in so much trouble. If only people would give—if 20,000 people gave $20 you'd have all of the house repaired, a car and what you needed for your business." THAT was Jerry.

He saw immediately the gift of giving and its impact if only people understood that one principle.

After we'd talked for a couple of years, his life changed, and he hit the skids after a divorce from a marriage that just didn't work out. He lived in Arizona where housing cost more than his paycheck.

For the first time in his life, he became homeless. It was devastating and thus began the roller coaster of his life for five years.

Still struggling from my own personal storm, it didn't stop me from trying to get help for him but sadly I could not get anyone's attention to help me do anything.

We developed a check-in system where he had to check in every day, regardless of the brutal sometimes twelve-to-fourteen-hour workdays at his job. His life became about finding safe places to park and going into the local Walmart bathroom to wash. He ate canned food out of his car and even in temperatures above 100 degrees in the summer, he persisted and did the best he could.

I began to send him audio messages filled with hope and then audio prayers, and later video prayers.

The first time I asked him if I could pray for him on the phone he said, "Just a minute, let me take off my cap and bow my head."

I would always reassure him that it wasn't his fault he was homeless. It wasn't.

Still in the midst of my own storm, he called one time, and this is what he said, "I don't know if God would hear my prayer, but this is what I said to Him."

I said, "What's that?"

He replied, "God, I ain't never met this woman but she lives for You better than anyone I know, and she is faithful. I think she deserves better than living in a place with holes in the floor, no running water, praying for food and clothes and a way to get down the road. Amen."

That's a prayer that opened the floodgate of tears that night.

Jerry was one of the most honest, hardworking people I'd ever known. It was important for him "to pay his own way" regardless of the situation he was in.

And he still dreamed and kept his dreams alive in whatever ways he could.

His life was more canned food, growing insomnia and then several runs to the emergency room.

Life was getting more and more complicated for Jerry.

He would always text me and ask about my day or my own personal storm that never seemed to end and always, always reassured me of his prayers for me. He DID pray. Always.

I tried (desperately!) to find him help, all to no avail but yet I persisted in praying for him every day, several times a day and the check-in's continued.

I often said about Jerry that if I had $22 million dollars in the bank, I would entrust it to his care, that he would never steal from me and if it was a penny off, he'd stay until he found the damn penny.

That was the Jerry I knew, also.

After several emergency room visits, his medical bills began to mount because of his deductible and life, for him, grew only more complicated and stressful.

Then one day I walked to the mailbox and saw his scribbled handwriting on an envelope. I thought, "What in the world is Jerry sending me?"

I opened the envelope and tucked inside a torn piece of notebook paper was a five-dollar bill.

Five Dollars from a Homeless Man.

I went inside the house and cried.

That five dollars became the reason for the title of this book.

And still, he would always tell me God would give me my miracles one day. He was the one who told me not to quit.

And despite his traumatic situation he would continue to believe in me and my dreams—and my writing—and that if anybody could get a miracle, I could.

As time went by (early 2024), he went to the ER because he went blind in his right eye. Tests didn't seem to reveal a diagnosis as to the "why" behind the blindness.

I begged him to go back to that ER—to any ER and find out why he was blind in that eye. He'd been diagnosed with high blood pressure time and again.

He wouldn't go. I still kept begging him to go and not risk his life. He kept talking about the medical debt he couldn't pay, his sleepless nights and the long, grueling work hours and the toll it was taking on him to be homeless now for five years. It was a relentless, grueling, horrible five years for him. His diet became peanuts, crackers, soda and water from the local dollar store. Sometimes his texts were disjointed, didn't make any sense and without complete sentences—whether stress, insomnia or the grueling toll of life on the edge from the bitter curse of homelessness I do not know.

His life was spiraling out of control.

Still, I prayed night and day for this kind man whose homelessness was not his fault. Praying to God to send someone to help me so I could help him. No one ever did.

On August 2nd of this year (2024) Jerry turned 59. It was his birthday.

Three days before August 15th (2024) I texted him. No reply.

I texted again.

No reply.

I told my sister, "Something's wrong. This isn't like Jerry."

No, it wasn't.

After the third text, on the Saturday after the 15th, his phone came through with a text that said, "May I ask who you are?"

I responded in kind and explained who I was and my friendship with Jerry.

They texted again and this time said, "May I call you?"

I looked at my sister who was visiting and said, "This isn't good."

No, it wasn't.

The person on the other end of the text was his sister-in-law. She called and told me that Jerry passed on August 15th at his job. When the security guards checked at five o'clock that evening, he was still alive.

When they did their security check at nine o'clock that same evening, they found him dead at his desk.

His sister-in-law told me that I was the only person on his phone, and he was getting ready to text me when he died.

This is what his text said right before his passing. He was typing the words, "I am no longer homeless…" and he died right before he hit the send button.

Jerry is no longer homeless.

And he will never be homeless again.

I'm not sure I am supposed to know why he was homeless for five years, neither am I to ever know (I don't suppose) why he died.

However, I can tell you this. The world is such a better place because he lived, and **my** life is forever humbled and changed because of the kindness of this man who was my friend.

He had what I call "courage under fire" and an honor almost impossible to find. He kept his word. He prayed. He fought. He cared. He had honor. He had integrity. He had grit. He was kind and compassionate and cared about other people far more than he cared about, well, Jerry.

When this book was first written, of course, Jerry's story wasn't in it, and I always told him that a portion of the proceeds from this book would go to help get him off the street. It seemed as though this book met with its own struggles, some of which I never understood but now, I can tell you, I **do understand why it struggled and it seemed as though this book had to "wait".**

It was originally written before Jerry's death, and this is his story as much as it is mine—and the Lord's.

I couldn't write it without having the world know his story.

Jerry will live forever in this book and that is how it should be. He will find himself in print and his name in "lights" throughout the world.

Remember what I said about Jerry wanting to be in film?

I've made yet another promise to God, although I don't "see" how it will come to fruition, but I leave that in God's care.

Somehow this book must go into film, and I must tell God's story and Jerry's story.

I would ask you to find someone who is homeless and rescue them. You won't regret it. There are a thousand ways to help that homeless person.

Homelessness is a silent, yet vicious raging epidemic when people can't afford to live, their rent or mortgage is more than they make and as so many people know, "you're one paycheck away from the street".

It is my personal opinion that Jerry shouldn't have died. He deserved better. Like all of us, he deserved a better life, a home and a way to make his dreams come true.

So, he couldn't make his dream come true about film.

I can.

Someone who is homeless needs to know how much they are loved—by another person and by God.

We often entertain angels unaware (as the Bible says) and as noted in this book. You never really know who the person that enters your life just might be.

If you can find a five-dollar bill, please go share it with someone who is homeless. It's about more than that five-dollar bill—it's about its message, about hope and about the power of a five-dollar bill to change someone's life. The life you change just might be your own.

I wish I had an answer for "the why" so many homeless people, especially men, die on the street. This side of heaven I may never know.

I am grateful for the storm that brought me to the real Jesus and the storm that caused me to meet a man named "Jerry Sanders". He will live forever—he already does—up there from heaven's door and its like he was trying to tell me, "I am no longer homeless..."

No, he isn't. And he won't ever be homeless again.

Seek out a homeless person and make them your friend. You'll be glad you did. If they're sick, get them medical help—somehow, some way. If you can possibly find safe shelter for them, do that, too. Find a food bank to help them with food.

If you have the way to give them a home, by all means do it. You cannot outgive God. Ever.

I cry a lot for this simple, honest man who will never know a long life here on earth, who only knew heartache and despair and who always felt so lost but as I noted earlier in this book, I would tell him, "You may have been lost but you were never lost to God."

There is a reason, a divine purpose that Jerry and I became friends. He needed that light inside the darkness. He needed hope but he also needed to know he was loved. And he did. He needed to know that his life had value. And he knew that.

His light was a brilliant one—a shining star in a dark midnight.

We can all do something so please do what you can. You won't regret it.

The light from this man's friendship has been extinguished but only until I see him again—and I will see him again and when I do, I hope he comes running up to me and says, "I am no longer homeless. Thank you for what you did."

Rest in peace, forever, Jerry Sanders (August 2nd, 1965 – August 15th, 2024)

IN MY OWN WORDS

"Help me to show people who you really are, Lord."

I needed to be alone these days, to reflect and pause. I no longer defined my future by corporate mission statements and the rules of the world. I truly want to serve only you, God and do whatever you have called me to do.

"Slow down, little girl! Stop the running!" I had finally said no to the forces of evil and as a result, they held no power over me. I had stopped fleeing the scene of the crime and running from the shadows. The voices had ceased and the demons no longer existed.

In the coming days, I knew my life must become one of new meaning, to focus on the love of God and the love He has for all His children. I was saddened as I learned that so many people think God would not, could not, forgive their transgressions. You are a loving, forgiving God, Lord. Help people to see your love and your forgiveness. You are always ready to forgive us—regardless of what we've done. And you are the only one who can unlock the prison doors, still the damning voices and destroy the demons. You are the only one who always keeps your promises and perform what your word says you will perform.

In the warm cocoon of your love, you are ready to bridge the gap and remove the burdens, to send your love and the Blood of your Son to free us from the past that holds us captive. The only real freedom lies in you, Lord, and the holy, reverent blood of your Son.

Help me to put you first—above all things, and all people. Help me, God, to do what you would have me do. To walk with you no matter what the road looks like. Help me to understand that today is all I really have. Help me to turn my vision from yesterday and give it to this moment. With your help, if there is a tomorrow, it is one created by, and for, you. Help me to use each moment wisely.

Give me the wellspring of joy. Reside in me. Live inside me and flow through me. Flow through my voice. Flow through my words.

Flow through my eyes. Flow through my actions. The world will never see you or find you unless they can see you in the way I live!

Flow through my hands and the talents you have given me.

The unveiling of the sacred journey has changed me and in turn, the looking glass is not the same. I am forever changed by your unfailing love and the sacrifice made by your Son.

May I live with an open hand and an open heart. Oh God, I have lived too long with a clenched fist and a wounded heart.

It has taken me so very long to find you—it seems I've searched for you through an entire lifetime. Pray, Lord, don't let me ever lose you again! If I get lost, come and find me, your little child, the little girl who is now a woman—a free woman in you!

Where the journey leads from here, I do not know. I only know that you will carry me through what lies ahead. You have carried me through the wind, and through the valleys, to the top of the mountain. I have survived my hauntings, and the terror of my transgressions. The devil is no longer tap dancing on my soul.

My soul is filled with wholeness now because of you. You met me in the black abyss of my despair and lifted me up in your arms. You have humbled me so I might know gratitude and touched me with sorrow so I might know joy. You have risen with me in the moments of adversity and carried me to a new height and dimension.

In my affliction was borne strength and in my weakness I was made strong in you.

When my soul was imprisoned, you opened the gates and set me free.

I am a whole woman, a complete person now. I have finally confronted my demons and let them go.

As I look upon the blank pages of my life, I know not where the next chapter begins and ends...but you do! Help me to see through your eyes. I know that if I see through your eyes, I will only love. If I see through your eyes, your love will transcend the barriers and destroy the hate. That same love will move the highest mountain and cast out the roots of bitterness. How many of us cling to the long held moments of darkness only to miss the moments of freedom?

Give me your heart so that I might love fully and completely—with great abandon and unconditionally. Give me your hands so that I might remember the price your Son paid when the nails were driven into His hands. Give me your grace for all the times in my life when I can't see beyond the pain. Give me your touch so that I might feel your healing power. Give me your strength so that I can do through you what I could not do alone. Touch me, Lord, with your spirit so that I might desire to help the forgotten people, the case numbers, the homeless, the lonely and neglected of this world.

I have been a statistic, the case number, a file folder, a blurred face in a long line of deserted people. But it was in those moments—when it felt as though no one cared—in those moments when I could not see my way through the storm—here is where I found you. Thank you God, that somewhere sits a case folder, in a file with my name on it. That file is etched in the scarlet red blood of your Son. What a glorious gift it was—to find you when my life fell apart! I would not be writing this story without the travail and the tragedy and the hopelessness that filled my life. In every test there is a testimony. This one is mine—and so it is I thank you, Lord, for it. It has been my greatest honor to walk through that fire for you and your Son. What was it I said? Oh, yes, I am dancing on coals of fire with feet of steel! I have danced in dark places and sang in the midst of my sorrows. I am no longer afraid of the wind, Lord. Thank you for the wind. And for the avalanches. And the rain.

Let me drink from your cup, Lord, if only once, so that I might thirst to know more of you. Give me the honor and privilege of knowing my walk is for you—that whatever persecutions and judgements come—you will handle them—and those who attempted to thrust the arrow into my heart and soul.

Lord, there are so many people entrenched in hate. Love and hate cannot exist in residence together. Don't they know that? Give them a mirror and let the reflection illuminate you instead of the roots of bitterness entangling their souls.

There have been so many times, Lord, when I walked alone. I never cast my eyes toward heaven to find you. Oh Lord, I am so sorry! How could I have forgotten? But I'll not forget again! You are with me in every situation and in every circumstance. I walked alone because I chose to walk the journey without you. You did not abandon me, Lord. I abandoned you! Oh, God, how many times have I wept, knowing I did that to you! Thank you, God, that your mercy was extended to me. You watched over me when I wasn't paying attention. You saved my life—you and your Son!

Help me to show people who you are through my actions, Lord and help me to walk out what I believe—regardless of how difficult that walk may be. Help me to remember that it is not important what someone else believes about me—only what you believe. When my journey here has ended and the final chapter is written, I want to hear you say, "Well done, my child." Those are the only words that truly matter!

Lord, I have learned a lot about material possessions throughout this journey. The problem is not having the material possessions. It's what we do with them when we have them! Do we build a bigger house or feed the poor? Walk, Lord, among your people. Teach us, Lord, to heed your voice. We are a starving people, hungry for food and drink, for the body and the soul. When will they ever learn, Lord? When will we ever learn, Lord? Thank you again, that I lost my earthly possessions. It was a part of the journey and its lesson I will never forget. Help me to give your people food and drink. Help me to show them the way to their soul! You are the way, the truth and the life. You are the Alpha, the Omega, the Beginning and the End.

Help me to find, and remember, the child within! Help me, most of all, to remember whose child I am! I am blood bought because Jesus paid the highest price for me when He died on the cross. Help me to remember to fly the kite! Build the dream! Paint the canvas! Catch a shooting star! Sit on the swing at sunset! Take deep breaths, grateful for the air and the mystery of another day! Help me to rejoice in that which you have freely given!

Lord, watch over my words. They are my destiny and with amazing force and magnitude, they travel to their destination, settling into what they have been called to do. My mouth, Lord, can either be a blessing or a curse. Let it bless and not curse. Let my words be a well of life instead of the pit of death.

Lord, help me to become a person of truth—help me to tell the truth even when it isn't easy to do so. For in truth, I will find freedom. Help me to value truth and may I always seek your truth—not the world's. Your truth is the only truth that will ever matter.

When I falter and stumble, please pick me up. Help me to dust myself off and get back up again—as many times as it takes! And if I am weary and can't do it on my own, thunder from heaven and shout, "get up!" Help me to surrender to you so that I can truly let go and let you. Get me out of the way so I stop trying to direct traffic. You are far better at directing traffic than I will ever be!

May I not be blinded by the beckoning of this world. Help me to see man's goodness and pray for his faults.

May I not get lost in the trivial things of which this world is made. Does it really matter if the bed isn't made exactly right? If someone's effort is less than perfect, help me to look at the effort and not the imperfection. If something doesn't go my way, help me to remember that in your Grand Design of things, it doesn't matter. What matters, really, is whether or not I've been a better soul with each day I'm given.

Help me, God! I don't want to waste a moment of this gift of life you have given me. It is a precious commodity and I need to work for you—not for me!

When I can't see my way around the darkened room, turn on the light and help me to see your face and your purpose.

Whatever comes my way, help me to deal with it in grace—your grace.

Give me the ability to focus on you, Lord. If I don't get it right, give me a second chance so I can get it right!

If I make the wrong decision, just tell me to make a "U-turn"!

Please continue to give me laughter in my soul and in my heart. Help me to remember that there is nothing so drastic that I can't find the humor in it—with your help!

Pray, Lord, help me to let go of the closed doors and stop looking over my shoulders so I can find an open door and an open window! And give me the wisdom to know when I need to change the locks!

When I feel all alone—help me to remember that I'm not—nor will I ever be! You are always with me. Thank you for your hand over the heart of the lost child I once was. Thank you for fighting the battles when I didn't know how. And thank you for your answers when I was too weak to ask the questions!

Help me to change one person, one city, one nation, the world—with the words you have given me to write. You are my voice and please help me to use it.

Give me equality in my sight. Don't shortchange my vision. We are all the same in your eyes. Help me to remember that, Lord. Help me to forget the differences I perceive in someone else and to remember that "we are all created in your image." You don't look at our differences so why should we?

Don't let me look at someone's record. Let me look at a slate wiped clean by the precious Blood of Jesus. What matters is what you have done with their lives, not where they have been. You are the potter who molds the roughest clay.

Help me, Lord, to slow down! Show me how to quit living life in the fast lanes! Help me to appreciate the sunrises. The voice of a child. The sound of the rain's choreography on the roof. My mother's voice and the gift of her embrace.

The tears in my father's eyes on the day I gave him the gift of forgiveness. Let me remember, in gratitude, all you have given me, and help me to appreciate it while I have it. May I always remember that you are the one who has given me everything I have.

May I leave behind that which needs to be left behind. Help me to put it away and close the book. There's a new book with my name on it—it is the book of life—and the only one that matters.

Help me to write the chapters as you would have them written.

And thank you, Lord, for erasers. May I learn to forget that which I have forgiven. May I remember that my past, my transgressions and all of my mistakes have been erased by you. Remind me to erase!

Help me to remember that a critical spirit is an ugly spirit. Help me, Lord, so that I won't criticize another—I don't have the whole story—nor am I likely to ever have it. There are two sides to every story. And unless I have lived where another has resided, I really don't know what it's like.

Help me to appreciate the storms so I can rejoice in the rainbows.

Help me to practice kindness—in whatever proportion I can give it and help me to do it joyfully.

God, I want to be a giver! I am blessed to be a blessing. Give me open hands!

May I acknowledge that when I worry or fear, it's really simple. I don't trust you when I do that. And I don't want to let you down, Lord. You knew me before I was in my mother's womb, and you know what will take place in my life before I do. Every day has been ordained and predestined by you. Make sure I remember that, please!

I look upon the journey that lies ahead with great anticipation. I have a divine opportunity to paint a different canvas, to sing a new song, and to write a new chapter.

I am ever grateful to have found release from the agony.

I am eager to travel a new frontier and move into a higher calling. I am blessed to have been a statistic, a forgotten people. I had been immersed too long in the womb of ignorance, expecting that I was untouchable, but you had to touch me in order to reach me, Lord.

There have been immeasurable blessings behind the bends in the roads—those detours I haven't always understood.

Losing it all gave me my greatest gift, for it afforded me the opportunity to find the realness of you.

You are the God I can cry with and in so doing, I am confident of your comfort. I can always expect your strength to sustain me. You are the same God today that so long ago covered the tears of a little girl with your own. Dear God, it feels so good to be free from the running! "Run, little girl, run! I can hear you tell me! Run, little girl, run! Only this time run to Me!"

You have loved me to greatness through the molding of me into the likeness of your Son.

Whether I am struggling in adversity or rejoicing in triumph, you are with me.

When I cannot stand on my own two feet, you lift me up by your own strength.

May people come to understand that you are a street God—you are there on the street with every hurting soul, every misguided choice and every heartbreak and broken dream. You are in the homeless shelters. You are the God who resides under the bridges when the weather is so ruthless and cold, and the homeless don't know how they can keep warm. You are the warmth that brings them in from the cold. If only we can learn to live to give and give to live—we could eradicate homelessness, Lord, I know we could!

You are the God who stands in heaven and cries when an injustice is done and a life is taken at the hands of someone's bitter hatred and prejudice.

You are a highway God—with every stretch of the winding road, you are there. You are He who made the clouds and the rain and smoothes the treacherous roads we sometimes face.

You are the God of low places—if your people will but look up, they will find you in the valleys, in the hard places, in the gutters and the ghettos. Once they find you, they have found their way out—of the hard places, the gutters and the ghettos.

You are the way, the truth, and the life. The Alpha, the Omega, the beginning and the end. You are come that they might have life and have it more abundantly.

You are a God who sits at summits and cabinet meetings. You reside over the Congress and the nations of this world. You are the God who weeps when man hurts man. The answers never lie in man's ways but in your ways.

When a child is born, you are there and when someone dies, you are there, as your angels carry them home to a better place.

For every trouble, you are the answer. You are a God who takes pleasure in turning setbacks into comebacks.

You are the God who rises with His people in the morning and lies with them when they sleep. You are the God who watches over every broken spirit and wounded heart.

You have given your promises to a hungry, starving people—all they must do is read it, believe and receive it! It's theirs! Just ask! You said that! Just ask! Dear Lord, when will we learn? Just ask you! You are the Father of lights! You are the Father of grace! The Father of love and mercy! Oh merciful God, you are waiting for your people to come to you! When will they run for the refuge of your loving arms?

If only people would realize, God, that the outcome is already written in the scarlet red blood of Jesus. You wrote the greatest book ever written when you handed down your word, your promises and your covenant to your people. All people are your people, Lord. When will we understand that?

The sacred journey has, at times, been painful, but I have opened the Pandora's box and looked inside. I looked at the face in mirror to find the person within.

The voyage has been worth it. I cry, Lord, but my tears are for the forgotten ones, whose voices cannot be heard above the din of indifference and prejudice. Are we so busy looking at the river that we forget the man by the stream?

How many people must we turn our backs on before we follow the circle home? When will we stop being accosted, and blinded, by our differences, and see the harmony and oneness you intended?

We were never meant to be a divided people, yet we have allowed the spirits of strife and dissension to separate us from you. Anything that is not of you separates us from the love of God.

I have lived in secondhand places, on secondhand dreams and all around me, I have seen lives filled with despair, raw hope replaced with fresh hopelessness. But you are a God who takes secondhand dreams and turns them into the fulfillment of your precious promises.

When, Lord, when, will we stop waging wars and battles with the bitter roots of our hatred? Your people, your nations have been forgotten, lost in the heat of battle, in the heat of angry words and broken promises. To heal, to restore, is to come to the One whose promises will never be broken.

We have looked for the formulas and solutions in all the wrong places—you are the solution. You are the only answer.

When will we learn? When? When will we throw down the armor of judgment and bitter hatred and pick up the shields of faith and prayer?

We must change the inward man so we can enter into the strange cities and speak to a different people, giving them the bread of life so they can change—one person at a time.

Heal us, Lord. Heal your people! We are a starving people whose souls are not at rest, for we desire the words of life and truth.

Speak, my Lord, speak to the nations and the people of your universe. Wars are never won in the courtroom or on the battlefield. Instead, they are won on bended knees—in prayer to you!

Help us, Lord, to throw down the spears and pick up the arrows of love.

I have spent the greater part of my life trying to settle the dust, banish the fears and find my purpose, Help me to know it, and do it, Lord!

You have taught me, God, that nothing is ever black and white, for people are covered in shades of grey.

I am coming back from the edge, picking up the pieces and finding my way. I will write a different story now because of my passage. Help me to reveal your truth to the forgotten people and the ones entombed in their arrogance.

I am no longer above reproach. Neither am I above being touched by life. Thank God for that!

Because of where I have been, the road that lies ahead will have a different destination. I have searched my soul to find the real God I know you to be. I have found you in my tears, in the vortex of my anguish, in the silence and in the rain. When the pain was so great I thought it would consume me, your hand reached out and covered my heart. I have found you in the shadows, in the darkness and in the scars. Look, Lord, I bear those scars so proudly! Look at the colors of my soul! Look at the scarlet red running through my spirit!

The little girl is finally free! I am running the race at the top of the mountain, looking back at the forgotten people with love and generosity, compassion and the beauty of an open heart and an open hand. I could never have stayed behind in the bondage that dominated my life.

Thank you, God, that I am rising above what was—to greet what is. I have seen and felt the heartbeat, the pulse, the heart of God. I know the heart of God. I have felt the presence of the Son. Face to face, heart to heart, soul to soul. On the wings of angels, you have carried me through this sacred journey.

I do not mourn for that which is past but rejoice for what is today. You have given me your best gift—the gift of your Son.

The stones hurled toward me were worth it, Lord. Although my voyage has been much more than I imagined, it is filled with greatness at the powerful touch of a loving God who goes behind prison walls, terrors, unforgiveness and pain. You are the loving God who touches the heart and purifies the spirit.

I am a spirit woman. A woman whose transgressions have been cleansed. For the first time, I am walking in freedom. I suppose it looks as if everything is the same, but how could it be?

Little girl in the mirror! Where are you, little girl? I am no longer the little girl in the mirror! I am the woman in the mirror. I am the free woman in the mirror. I am a woman whose past was unhinged by the tremendous touch of a loving God who unlocked my chains and set me free.

I feel like running today, Lord! The air is so clear and I am drinking from the fountain of life. I have laid to rest the broken spirit and felt the touch of God and the Blood of His Son as He made whole that which was incomplete.

I am moving within the circle, dancing in the light of God's love, singing atop the mountain. Dear God, I am free! Make your people free! You want to set them free! Come out of the prisons! Come out of the bondage! Let go of the hatred! We are all one in your eyes, Lord!

These days, in these moments blessed by you, my eyes are no longer darting to and fro, looking for the answers, trying to figure out what will happen next. You have written the book, and you know the plan. You are the architect and you have designed my life and everything that will happen.

I have learned so much throughout this journey that I know is not yet ended—there are so many more miles to travel and many more stories to be written. You will help me write them. The darkness has been one of my greatest lessons.

Too many people, God, are cast aside in this life we lead. They are ignored by others and left to their own aloneness. Why, God, can't everyone figure out that if we would just love and help each other, the whole world would change? We need to become a listening people, a loving people, a giving people. We must hear not what we want to hear but instead, we must open our ears to the truth. Our people, our nations, and our lands will never change until they learn, God, who you really are. You are the God of the white man, the red man, the yellow man, the black man—and all men. The scarlet red threads are running through your people if only they knew it. Your love is not divided and set only for a chosen few. Your redemption is for everyone who will receive it.

Our thoughts become words and our words become actions, setting in motion the force of our destiny. I have learned to think on things of you and to think in the spirit. I am not measured by the world's standards nor do I want to be. It is enough to be measured by you. I love you, God. You are my Father. I have learned to find the soul of my fellow man instead of looking for the superficial exterior.

We are all your people—pray, Lord, when will we ever learn?

I have learned to ride the wind and climb the mountains—thanks to you, Lord. I am no longer embittered but empowered.

I sat again along the sand dunes and looked at the silver cross and the notebook filled to overflowing with the words you have given me. My cup runneth over. After all the years spent in hiding, I am drinking from the cup of life and running toward the joy of eternal life.

I have emerged from the games of playing hide and seek! I am no longer on the search and rescue mission for my soul.

It is not finished—not yet—this sacred journey I have begun. I have much to do for you. Help me to do it, God. Help me to be your voice, Lord!

I am giving a final glance to my past—to the broken spirit and wounded heart, the unrealized dreams and the haunted soul I once was. I am saying goodbye to the girl who started this quest and opening the door to my future, to the world that lies ahead, and the woman I have become. I have become a free woman because of you, God. You stood in the gap of my emotional minefield as your tears washed over my own and the Blood of your Son covered my soul. I am washed in His Blood and covered in the river of your tears. You loved me so much you gave your only begotten Son. You wanted me to leave behind the torment of my life. You wanted me to come to the river of life. I'm here, God. I've finally come to the river—and to the mountain. Let us not forget where I've been. If I forget, I won't help someone else chained in their own private purgatories and prisons. You are the gatekeeper. You opened the gate and bid me come. Come to me! Follow me! I am with thee!

With every pain that assaulted my soul, you were there, saying, "Look up, little girl, to the one who loves you!" When I battled my fears and fought to get out of the chains, you said, "Fear not, I am with you! I will come and help you!"

Somehow, I have always known that you would be faithful to finish that which you started in me.

You spoke to me again and said, "Loose the chains and set yourself free! The gate is open!"

Sometimes I wonder, "How will I ever thank you, God?" Peace resides where once there was war. I am fulfilling the circle. I am finding my way. I am answering your call on my life. I am no longer a broken woman, for you have restored and repaired that which was broken—I have found the answers in you.

THE MAN ON THE BENCH 87

Where are we going, Lord? I don't really know but then, I don't have to know. Where ever we go, we're going together.

Thank you for giving my life back to me. For giving me my mother and helping me to embrace my father. His sins will no longer reside in me. Thanks to you, God!

Thank you, God, for being with me in all of those dark moments. And thank you for turning on the light when I couldn't find the switch!

I have found honor in my soul because of you, God and there are no ample words of gratitude for that, Lord. You and I have entered into a blood covenant—a covenant of promises and honor, bought by the holy blood of your Son.

Dear God, I am finally free! I looked up and the winds changed again. Was it because I have changed? You are with me in the wind and rain. Let us continue on, Lord, to the top of the mountain.

As I walked along the ocean's shores, I felt the presence of your love, Lord. Freedom is a priceless gift. Freedom that only you can bring. Thank you for the keys to the kingdom. I am grateful to have found your heart, Lord, the heart of God.

The unveiling of the sacred journey will continue and I will learn, and grow and change. But I will do it with your hand in mine. I will carry your message to the world and when the curtain closes, and the angels stand ready to carry me home to you, perhaps you and I will simply say, **"To be continued—"**

CASSIE LIGHT REDFEATHER is author of THE PROSPERITY GOSPEL and THE HAUNTING OF ALYSSA.

Did you love *The Man on the Bench*? Then you should read *The Prosperity Gospel*[1] by Cassie Light Redfeather!

[2]

My journey started long ago when I stared at the camera and the preacher on the other side of the camera lens. Prosperity was preached 24 hours a day anytime I turned on the television. Miracles, however, are not for sale. Why was the preacher rich but his flock wasn't? Struggling in the midst of adversity and setbacks I began to question the Prosperity Gospel. This is my story of the journey from the Prosperity Gospel to prosperity and wealth that can only come from the Lord.

---

1. https://books2read.com/u/3LqaXJ

2. https://books2read.com/u/3LqaXJ